# PETEY AND THE BEAR

by Susan Newman-Harrison
with illustrations by Stefan Strasser

Written by: Susan Newman-Harrison
Illustrations by: Stefan Strasser

Library of Congress Control Number: TXu 2-150-381

ISBN 978-1-7337293-0-7

# PETEY AND THE BEAR

Dedicated to my husband
Rob Harrison
"The Tumbling Bear"

— Susan Newman-Harrison

There was a Bear that worked away every day all alone on projects. No one ever came to visit or help the Bear. He was busy and had much to accomplish all the time.

One day, he saw little animals from the distance, and quickly noticed there were two of them. They looked so happy playing around. The Bear wished he had a little animal like them to play with.
But, they were far away, and the Bear kept on working because while the sun was shining, he had to work. He went home at night to rest, and always returned to his workshop the next day.

The next morning, as the sun was rising, the bear was stretching and quickly realized, it's time for him to get to work. "I must work hard today to finish my projects," said the Bear.

As he got to his workshop, he looked for those two beautiful little animals, and there they were, playing and all happy. He would watch them from a distance, smile and then go back to work.

The Bear worked away, and kept thinking about those two little happy animals. He didn't know exactly what they were. When he finished one of his projects, the Bear decided to take a walk and see what they were. Oh my, they were two little kittens. One was named "Tassie" and one was named "Petey." They looked very much the same, one could barely tell them apart. So the Bear played with them and they were so happy they found a new fuzzy bear friend to play with.

One morning, the Bear got to the workshop, and noticed there was only one little kitten in the distance. It was Petey. He seemed so sad. He was looking to the west, toward the mountains, far away. The Bear walked over and asked, "Petey, why do you look so sad?" Petey said, "I've lost my sister, she's gone west and no one has seen her."

The Bear hugged Petey and said, "I am sorry your sister has gone west. Maybe she will return and one day you will see her again. Petey, I will be your new friend. I will visit you and play with you. I will let you ride in my workshop cart. I will even get a nice soft pillow for you. Don't worry Petey, when I go fishing on the lake, I will catch a nice fish for you."

Petey was happy he had a new friend! He said, "Thank you, Mr. Bear. I really needed a friend."

The Bear and Petey shook hands and agreed they would be friends forever.

Every morning when the Bear came to the workshop, he would wave hello to Petey. One day, Petey decided to walk down to see what the Bear was working on.

Petey was amazed as he looked around and saw all what the Bear was building. Petey asked, "What is this, Mr. Bear?"

Mr. Bear said, "Well, Petey, have a seat. I will tell you about this project and one day, you will see how it works." Petey was happy and rested next to the Bear while he listened to his stories.

"Well my friend Petey, you see, people say animals are not smart and that only birds and some oh some squirrels are the only ones that can fly. They say that Bears can't fly. But, you see, I am building what is called a flying machine. And I will show the people that Bears do fly. I know, well, I will sit inside the flying machine and fly it in the air."

Petey said, "Really Mr. Bear, really!? Can I go with you?" And the Bear smiled and said, "Sure Petey, you can always fly with me. But, for now, you can keep me company while I work away and one day, we will fly this machine." "Oh goodie, I can't wait!" said Petey.

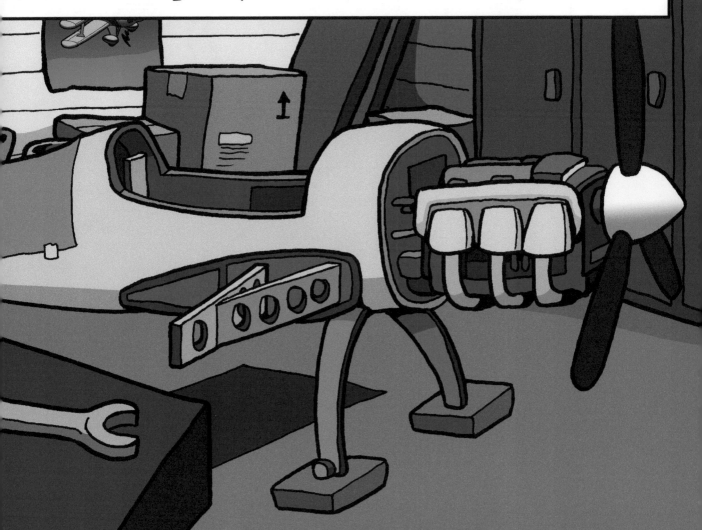

Every morning, Petey would listen for Mr. Bear's arrival. He would go visit the Bear and give him a hug. And help him and sometimes just sleep and watch him. At times, the Bear had trouble making parts for the flying machine, and felt sad, but Petey always cheered him up and he continued to work hard because Petey was there with him.

Petey would keep the birds and mice out of the Bears workshop because he knew the flying machine was made of silk and the mice liked to eat the silk and the wires. So, Petey worked hard too, and kept the workshop nice and clean for the Bear. And, sometimes, Petey would just take a nap and kept his Bear friend company.

On a cold evening Mr. Bear said, "Petey, why don't you come to my cave tonight? I heard the stormy clouds were rolling in and the night will be cold."

Petey was happy and went home with the Bear. They had a nice firepit and cooked fresh fish on an open fire. Petey never had so much fun.

The next couple of months, they worked very hard on the flying machine. It was time to go flying! Mr. Bear gave Petey a hat to wear and goggles to protect his eyes. They jumped in the flying machine, and up, up, up and away they climbed into the sky. They were both giggling and laughing. Petey said, "No one will ever believe we were flying! A bear? A cat? Flying? Oh no, no one will believe us!"

Every morning, the Bear went to his workshop and made the flying machine better and better and he was so happy he could take his friend Petey flying up in the sky.

The Bear was busy and told Petey to keep an eye around the workshop for him while he was away fetching supplies for the flying machine. Days went by, and Petey was lonely and missed the Bear. He couldn't wait until the day the Bear returned.

On an early morning, the Bear returned to the workshop and called for Petey. He walked around and around and found no sign of Petey. He walked back to his workshop and cried. "I miss my friend Petey. My workshop will never be the same. It's very quiet and lonely here." So, the Bear closed the workshop doors and went home.

Days went by, and the Bear went to the workshop, and no Petey. He would call him and then cry. "What am I going to do? I really miss my friend. I can't fly this machine without my friend! Petey! Where are you Petey!? Please come back Petey."

But, no Petey.

So, the Bear went home. Didn't eat and went to sleep. He was very very sad and missed his friend Petey.

At midnight, he woke up and said, who's holding a light to my eye? Oh, no one, it was the moon. The Bear rubbed his eyes and said, what is that in the sky? Is that the flying machine? Who's in my flying machine?

"Mr. Bear, Mr. Bear, it's me, Petey! Wake up! I've been looking for you!

Mr. Bear woke up and waived his arms and said, "Come get me Petey! I'm right here." So, Petey landed the flying machine and said, "Jump in Mr. Bear let's go for a ride in the sky. We will fly to the moon!"

Mr. Bear didn't realize that all those hours they spent in the workshop, Petey had been paying attention and had learned to fly.

"Oh Petey, you are my best friend. Thank you for looking for me. I was very sad and I missed you," said Mr. Bear. And, Petey said to Mr. Bear, "I always look after you. We are best friends forever."

And, as the moon lit the sky, Petey and Mr. Bear flew around laughing and having a good time until the morning sun came out.

CPSIA information can be obtained
at www.ICGtesting.com
Printed in the USA
BVHW021711160821
614548BV00003B/23